WHEN YOU CAN'T LET GO

DAMAGED LOVE SERIES BOOK 1

MIA BLACK

CHAPTER 1

Jericka

"No touching," I said. I tried to make it sound sexy but in all honesty, I was annoyed. I didn't need any niggas touching me and trying to grab me. I hated that shit. I rolled my eyes but he couldn't see it. His eyes were on my ass. I could feel them there. In fact, I'm sure his fat ass hadn't even looked me in my face once since the night began.

He was sitting in the chair behind me. I was almost a little surprised that it could hold him up cause he was so fat but whatever. I turned around so that he was face to face with me. I grabbed my breasts in my hands and then grabbed his hands. I pulled his hands up to my chest like I was about to let him touch them then I stopped and put them back down on his side.

I turned back around and started maneuvering my hips so that I was grinding on his dick...or where his dick should have been. I'd done enough lap dances to pretty much be able to tell when a guy was working with something nice or not and this dude definitely wasn't. I wasn't interested in him like that though so it didn't even really matter to me what his dick looked like.

"Ok ma, I got you," he said with a deep breath. I felt his warm breath on the small of my back as I kept moving my body. "Just keep moving." I heard his hands drop to the armrest of the chair behind me. "You so pretty."

I was pretty, too. That was why on most nights I was able to usually get a couple more dollars than the average chick in the strip club. At 24 years old, I was 5'4" tall, a little more petite than some but I made up for my lack of height in other ways. I had smooth, milk chocolate colored skin that was clear and looked really smooth with or without makeup. And I wasn't the type who usually wore makeup. I had a weave that came down to the middle of my back that was the color of red wine, deep and dark. Don't get it twisted though, I had my own hair and it was long; I just hated all the maintenance of it sometimes. Besides, working in the strip club wasn't about me being me. It was about me selling the fantasy of it all. These niggas loved long weaves and thick asses. My Southern roots had given me all the thickness I ever needed: a thin waist and flat stomach that led down to thick thighs and a fat ass. I tried to workout whenever I could so that I could stay in shape but I also got enough workout having to do all those tricks and shit on a pole. There was nothing worse than a flabby stripper, unless that was your kind of thing, in which case if you liked it, I loved it.

"Whatever you say boo," I said. The words came out of my mouth with disgust and he didn't even catch it, not that I would have cared.

I bent over in front of him, my ass jiggling in front of his face as I wiggled my thighs to make my ass move even more. Niggas loved stuff like that. I still had on my thong though. It was really rare for me to actually get all the way naked for a lap dance for two reasons. The first was that I could make my body move so good that by the end of the dance, these niggas didn't care what I was wearing. The second was that very rarely did anybody tip enough for me to really wanna get naked. I wasn't one of those bitches who enjoyed stuff like this. This was more survival than anything.

I turned my body around and looked up into the mirror behind him. I loved the red lighting of the room. It made everything feel sexier, even when you had ugly niggas like this guy in front of you. I grabbed my titties up in both of my hands, not that they needed any help; they stood up good on their own. I held them in my hands before making a move and taking off my bra without reaching behind my back. Dudes loved when I did that. His grubby hands threw a couple of dollars into the air and smirked at me like he was doing something.

Nigga, that's not even enough for a cab ride home, I thought. Not that I needed a cab since I had my own car.

I rolled my eyes. Being a stripper was a lot of work and I thought people would be surprised if they knew all the shit that went into it. When you were on stage you had to deal with men thinking they were buying you, throwing dollars and expecting you to do whatever they wanted. With the way that the world of stripping had grown over the years, it wasn't that easy to make a dollar anymore. People were expecting you to do all types of shit: hang from ceilings, make your ass clap, kiss girls, and all this other shit on top of it all. When I first got into the game it was different and that wasn't even that long ago.

The part that was usually hit or miss for me though was always the private lap dances. Guys thought they were renting you and I had to remind them that all the time of the rules: no touching, when you stop tipping the dance is done, all that shit. Sometimes the tips were really good and other times I wondered why I kept coming in to work. I was tired of the living the life of stripper. I really just wanted to just enjoy my family but with everything going the way that it was going, I guess I just had to keep it going for a little while longer, hopefully.

The name of the fat fuck I was dancing for was Dave. He was in his early 40's and was brown skinned and overweight. He had a mole on the side of his cheek, bushy eyebrows, and was going bald but hadn't made the decision to just cut it all off yet, which I just couldn't understand. The worst part of it all was that he had some of the worst breath I'd ever smelled. It smelled like a mixture of fish sticks and shit. Every time he came to talk to me, I wanted to tell him that he needed go to the dentist to get his mouth checked out cause there was definitely something wrong in there. The strangest part of the whole thing with Dave was that somehow he was married. I didn't understand how though cause it seemed like he spent almost every day in the strip club, throwing money at women.

I backed my ass up on him a couple more times. I took a shot right before I came into the room with him. I needed it in order to get through the dance. I liked drinking but I didn't do it too often at work cause I always needed to be alert when I was at the club. I'd seen a lot of crazy shit happen and I wasn't trying to be the next story on the news or talk of gossip.

I finished my dance with Dave. I picked up my money and did a quick mental count. Eighteen fucking dollars. It wasn't even worth my time. Thankfully I'd gotten a little bit of money up front from him too. He had to pay for the dance and everything else was just tips. I'd seen that movie *The Players Club* a bunch of times but I never thought that I'd be living that shit. I stood up and turned around, about to pull the curtain back and walk out. I opened it and was about to leave when I felt something tap me on my ass. Nasty ass Dave.

"Don't you fuckin touch me!" I said. I was making sure I made sure I sounded serious. These niggas be getting out of hands some-times. "I'm serious too. I'll tell Rashid, Tay, and all the rest of the guards not to let your fat, funky ass up in here no more."

He sat back in his chair and held his hands up. "My bad, Raven," he said. He looked apolo-getic. I just sucked my teeth.

With that I threw the curtain all the way back. I was getting sick of the shit. Stripping had never really been what I wanted to do with my life but it was something for me to get into because I had people in my life that I needed to support.

Jehovah "Hov" Gardner, better known to the streets and to me as Hov was the man I loved and he was the reason that I was working in a strip club. I'd love to be able to tell you that it was because he was the owner of the club or something fancier than what the truth actually was. I guess it was true what they said: sometimes the truth is stranger than fiction.

Hov and I had met one another when we were younger. I was 17 years old when he and I first crossed paths. Of course at that age I thought I had shit figured out. I was fresh outta school for the summer and had a head full of dreams and ideas. I was ready to take over the world for two months until I went back for my final year of school.

I remembered the first time I saw Hov. It was July 4th weekend and I'd let my best friend, Tamika, talk me into going to the beach. Chicago wasn't near an ocean or anything but we had Lake Michigan and it was where everyone hung out with during the summer. My mother had moved us from Atlanta to Chicago and she was always working but she checked in with me all the time to make sure that I was doing the right thing.

Tamika told me that she'd heard about a party that was supposed to be lit so we wanted to check it out. I managed to get time off from whatever job I was working at the time and we headed out.

The party was fun, better than I thought it was gonna be. The party was out on the actual beach but the whole crowd had kind of sectioned off one part as our own. I remember that when I first looked at Hov, I realized he was probably one of the most handsome boys I'd ever seen. He grew into an even more handsome man.

Now, I'd heard things on the street about Hov and his crew. I knew that they were making a name on the street for themselves as some little dough boys. I couldn't front, it was exciting to see him in person. He asked me to dance with him and we danced for what seemed like forever. The thing I liked about him the most at first was that he seemed to be fearless. You know how hood dudes can be: too cool to do anything, always serious and stuff like that.

"Yo," said Hov. *He approached me slowly. He was only 18 but I knew he was something special even then. He didn't carry himself the same way as others. He moved like an old soul, like there was some kind of secret*

that only he knew about. I loved it cause it made him look even more mysterious to me.

"What's going on?" I greeted him. Tamika was standing there talking to some boy but my girl could multi task so I'm sure she was all up in my mouth trying to catch every word I was saying, even though she knew I'd tell her about it later on.

"You not from around here, are you?" It was a question but he said it like it was a statement. I'm sure he already knew the answer.

"Nah, I stay on the North side," I said. "You?"

"Southside all day baby," he said. He must have realized it was kind of corny cause he smirked after. I did too. "You wanna dance?"

I was still smiling. "I don't know," I said. "My mother told me not to talk to strangers so I don't think I can dance with them either."

"I'm Hov," he said. He said it in such a way that must have been waiting for me to be surprised or something.

"Cool. I'm Jericka," I said.

I knew from the first day that we met that Hov was something special. He wasn't afraid to do simple shit like dance and laugh too loud for no reason. I took things really slow with him that summer. I wasn't about to be some groupie or something like that. People really be out here sweating drug dealers and I was playing it cool. I needed him to know that I would be good with or without him. Besides, I was only 17 years old. I wasn't thinking about the future like that. I wanted someone to chill and go to the movies with.

We finally got together that fall right before I went back for my last year of high school. I was happy to finally have somebody for me. On Christmas night, I let Hov take my virginity. I'd known that he had been dying to do it and I finally decided that it was worth it and that I could trust him.

After I graduated, I moved in with Hov. My mother wasn't a fan of it at all. I had to talk to her and let her know that she'd raised me right. I know it wasn't in her plan for me to move in with some drug dealer or anything but after she met Hov, she chilled out. She knew that she'd raised me to make the best decisions possible. Not to mention that she still had to take care of my little brother. When Hov finally got on top, he threw my mother some money. I made sure my lady was taken care of, even though she never really spent the money. Hov been living on his own in this cool little spot, and at first, we clashed a little bit. I don't think either of us really knew how to live with someone we loved but we figured it out. I liked being with him because he knew how to treat me and made me happy. I held him down too. I played my position and took care of him and home. We made the transition from kids to adults with one another.

Over the years Hov's little corner thing grew until he wasn't just someone small time. He had a whole drug empire and he was good at running it. Hov pretty much took over the Southside of Chicago. His name held weight on the streets and I reaped the benefits of the money: cars, a house, shopping whenever I wanted, the works.

We were living out hood dreams. Hov moved us up out of that tiny one bedroom and eventually took us to a nice ass condo. We had it all, money, cars, clothes, all of that. Hov took care of home. I never had to go out and get a job. He was cool with me staying home and taking care of shit for him. All of his friends knew me and knew that I was his ride or die and that I had his back. I learned the hard way that the saying "the bigger they are, the harder they fall" is true. Hov's shit was bigger than life so it was heartbreaking to watch shit crumble with us.

I wish I knew what it was that triggered the change in him. About two years ago, Hov broke one of the biggest rules of the drug game: never get high on your own supply. I first noticed something was wrong when I smelled him smoking a blunt and the shit smelled different. I asked him why it smelled like that and he said that he added a "little something extra."

One day I came home and found out that he was dusting—making blunts and then sprin- kling them with coke. I was shocked. I asked him about it and he said that some bitch had put him on to it. I found out later on that they'd fucked once or twice behind my back. I was hurt by it but I stayed. We had a son together and I thought that his problem wasn't a problem.

Over time I've watched Hov become a shadow of who he used to be. He could walk into a room and just fill it with his presence, but now he was just a fuckin' addict. I wasn't even sure of how many drugs he was doing. All I knew was that after a while, I had to use the little money we had saved to pay the bills. Then I found out that he wasn't paying the mortgage so our lavish condo got snatched right from under us. I used the last of my savings to get us into a two-bedroom apartment and pay some of the rent in advance. All the shit that he had before was gone—the money, the friends, the cars, all of it.

I thought that watching our life crumble right before our eyes might be enough to snap him from his addiction, but it didn't work. When we moved into our new spot, he had all these promises. We had to downgrade to a tiny ass two-bedroom apartment. It was barely bigger than the first place we'd lived. He said he was gonna get clean and get a job or go back to hustling. I was happy when he went to rehab the first time but he soon relapsed. Hov had been to various rehab places over the years but he always went back to the drugs. I couldn't compete with the monkey on his back.

I know a lot of people might look at my situation and wonder why I was still with him but I did have my own reasons. I loved Hov. He was the man who I'd been through a lot of shit with. I couldn't just turn my back on him. He needed me because he was going through something. I loved him regardless of anything. All the stuff that we had before was just material stuff. In the back of my mind though, I felt like the time might be coming for me to just leave him alone and let him get himself together.

The other main reason I stayed with Hov was simple: our son, Jasheem Gardner. He was our little baby. He was 5 years old and loved both me and Hov. I always wanted for my child to grow up with both parents. I hoped that things with Hov got better so that that could be a reality. When I got pregnant with Jasheem, my mother was surprised cause she thought that I'd have been pregnant already. When I told Hov, he got all emotional and stuff. The day that I gave birth, I'd almost killed Hov in the delivery room. Being pregnant was more problematic than I thought it would be and giving birth was some next level shit.

With our new circumstances, Hov didn't work. Every now and then he might bring in a couple of dollars somehow but I was the one who brought in the real money. I didn't want to get into stripping but it was the easiest way for me to make money. I had the curves for it. We got into debt right after we moved into the new place so I needed cash in a hurry. I realized that stripping was the easiest way to get it. Tamika had told me that she thought I could make a lot of money doing it.

I was annoyed as I walked back to the dressing room. There were nothing but broke ass dudes in the club that night. Slow wasn't even the fucking word. I needed to get more money. I knew that Hov would've probably blown through his little stash already. I didn't need him coming at me trying to 'punish' me for not bringing in enough money. I hated that most of what I made went up his nose or into his arm. Something had to give.

I never thought that shit with Hov would get as bad as it had become. About a year ago was the first time he'd ever hit me. He and I were arguing. He'd gone into my bag and taken the money I had set aside for the light bill. He claimed that he'd be making it right back and was only borrowing it. I told him that the lights would be cut off in the morning unless the bill got paid so he needed to get the money back ASAP.

He and I kept arguing and going back and

forth with one another. I yelled something at him and he slapped the shit out of me. Hov was bigger than me. He was 5'11" with skin the color of caramel. Hov always had an imposing look about him. He was solidly built with muscles and had tattoos all over his body. He had a bald and a full beard that he kept groomed, no matter what. Before he had been an addict, he had bitches chasing after him, and he still had them now. Hov wasn't the type of guy to let himself look crazy. He made sure that he kept his drug use on the low, only letting a few people know about it. What he didn't know though was that way more people knew than he thought. I wonder if any of them would want him if they knew what he was up to.

After the first time he hit me, he apologized and stuff. I was so shocked that all I could do was cry. Shit was going fine for a long time and then it happened again. Before I knew it, it was an almost like I could predict when it would happen again. After each time, Hov would apologize and tell me it was never going to happen again. I knew now that I shouldn't hold my breath waiting for that day to come. Hov would break down and cry, saying he needed help. He begs me not to take his family away from him. He begged me not to leave. I always forgave him because I knew how much family meant to him.

When you're growing up and hear bitches talk about abusive relationships and shit, you never think it's gonna be you. If you would have told me that Hov would hit me more than once or that I would have stayed, I would have said you were drunk or something. But there I was.

I hung around the club for another two hours. I was pissed off because I'd only made a little over $400. It was annoying because on a good night I could make that much in an hour. Every night before I left I always had to do some mental math. I needed to figure out how much money to give Hov and how much to set aside for bills and other things that needed to be taken care of around the house.

I got dressed and headed out. It was a little after 3 in the morning. I spotted one of the guards, Tay, out in the parking lot.

"Get home safe Jericka," he said. My stage name was Raven but I let certain people call me by my real name, Jericka. It made it feel friendlier. I found it beneficial to be friends with the guards and shit. They held parking spots for me and shit.

"You too, Tay," I said. I hopped into my little hooptie, another sign of the downgraded life I was living. I drove off, headed home. I wouldn't get there until 4 in the morning. I'd only be able to get a few hours of sleep since I had to be at my mother's house at 9 to pick up Jasheem.

CHAPTER 2

Hov

"Fuck outta here with that shit yo," I said as I busted out laughing. That nigga James was a fucking clown. We were chilling at my house and he was telling me a story about some bitch he supposedly fucked. That was James for you—that nigga always had a story to tell.

"Nah yo," he said, trying not to laugh as he kept on going with his story, "I'm dead ass Hov. This bitch was doing shit you never seen before." He mimicked himself throwing somebody up into the air and catching them. I kept on laughing. He was crazy.

"Nigga please. Ain't nobody gonna be fucking with your ugly ass like that," I said as I busted out laughing once again. The look on that nigga's face was priceless. James hated it when people called him ugly. He said he was an ugly kid who grew into his looks but I think my boy still had some growing to do if he didn't wanna be ugly anymore.

"Ha ha, very funny," he said. He reached into his pocket and pulled out a little baggie. He held it between his thumb and pointer with one hand and flicked it with the other. My eyes got all wide and I felt my mouth begin to twitch just at the side of the bag. I hated how much of an affect I let that shit have on me. I knew I needed to quit and I knew that one day I would.

"Yeah, exactly," he said. "Talkin' all that shit but you bout to ask me for a hit."

"Fuck outta here," I said. The truth was that I did want a hit and we both knew that I had every intention on asking for one, no matter what I'd just said.

My own little stash was low. If I remembered correctly, I realized that I only had enough left for one more high. I definitely wasn't about to split that shit with James. I was gonna get high as hell later on but it would be good to get a little sampler from his shit.

"Whatever," he said. He opened the bag and poured the contents out onto the coffee table. He reached for a playing card on the table and began to cut the small pieces into smaller pieces and then separate them into lines. He made 4 lines, two for each of us. We'd just done two lines like an hour and a half ago but fuck it, I wanted to keep my high going.

"So you want some or what?" James asked. I looked into his eyes and saw the same look of hunger in them that I knew had to be in mine too.

I wasn't a crackhead. Yeah, I'd done crack a couple of times...maybe more than a couple of times actually. I kinda liked coke more though. It all depended on my mood. Crackheads were niggas that stole toasters and shit for money. Crackheads nodded off on corners and shit. I wasn't that at all. Yeah I did drugs or whatever but if you looked at me you'd never be able to tell. I made sure that I only bought my shit on the low and only from the same person. Niggas will see you out copping that shit and automatically try and label you like you addicted to that white girl. That wasn't me.

"Hell yeah," I said. He scooted to the side and let me sit in front of the table. I leaned down and held one nostril and inhaled deeply with the other. I took a couple of deep breaths and did the same again, watching the other line vanish as I sniffed. I went back to my side of the couch and sat back with my eyes closed. I heard James sniff too and when I opened my eyes, his lines were gone.

I felt everything as I leaned back on the couch. I felt my heart beat faster and faster. I felt my whole body tingling and I felt like I was flying, even though I knew that I was still sitting down on the couch. I loved that feeling. My mind was moving quick as hell, just thinking about everything and nothing all at the same time.

Jericka crossed my mind. I hope she wasn't playing no games later on whenever she came in. I needed some more money. My stash was low and it needed to be refilled. She left saying that she felt like it was gonna be a good night. I hoped it was. Jericka didn't need no problems with me.

I drifted off to sleep and woke up a little while later. I looked at my phone. It was a little after 11. James was gone. I didn't hear him in the bathroom which meant he'd probably left to go fuck some next bitch for his next story. I laughed out loud at that.

I was coming down off my high. I hated that feelings. I liked being high cause it made me forget about shit. The first time I got high I felt like a fuckin superhero. I felt like Superman or some shit. I was flying high above every- thing...all the good and the bad. Since then I've been trying to get back to that point but I can't really reach it.

I also hated coming down off my high because it meant that I was coming back down to my thoughts and shit. Nobody understood how I felt and I got high cause it made me not deal with it at all.

I used to be on top of the world. Niggas on the street could say the name Hov and people would automatically know that they had to put some respect on my name. I had the streets locked down and made sure that niggas knew it. I ran my crew with an iron fist. I was tough but still fair at the same time. I showed my niggas loyalty that a lot of other people lacked and shit.

As a result of me doing all the shit I did, I had it all. I was living in a nice ass 3-bedroom condo with my baby mother and girlfriend, Jericka and our son Jasheem. We had shit that niggas only dreamed of: doorman, multiple cars, top of the line electronics, jewelry, the whole works. We were living a street dream for real. It was all going good till I let my little problem get in the way.

It felt like Jericka was my good luck charm. Right after I got with her was when my shirt went from small time to big time. She was there with me every step of the way, being everything a ride or die should be. She made sure that she held me down in every way that she could. In return, I showered my baby with everything I could: jewelry, cars, clothes, love. She didn't have to work. She was on the verge of starting a little business for herself when shit started to go left for us.

I had good times with Jericka though. She

was really special. She'd only ever been with me and I loved that about her. Too many of these bitches in the street had been ran through by a couple of people. I'd fucked up a couple of times and fucked around behind her back but she knew that I knew where my home was. Her and Jasheem were really all I had and I wasn't about to let that go for nobody.

We were young when we first got together. She was fresh outta high school. I would have been too if I didn't drop out. I was a child of the streets and they always called my name. I made a way for myself and made sure that I was good. Before I let Jericka move in with me, I had to make sure I could trust her. Once she'd proven her loyalty, she moved in and shit was cool. We fought a lot in the beginning but it was a part of the growing process. We were kids still and didn't really have many plans and shit. We just knew we wanted to be together and that was it.

Shit was so crazy for real. For the rest of my life I'd never forget the moment I brought Jericka and Jah into the new spot. I was carrying Jasheem and I put a blindfold onto Jericka. I wanted her to be surprised. She wasn't a big fan of surprises but I managed to convince her. She was down with it.

Once I told her to take off the blindfold, she was confused and then surprised. Jericka asked where we were and once I explained to her that we were in the living room of our new home, she got down on her knees and cried tears of happiness. I knew then that I could really be with her for life and shit. I knew Jericka loved me, even though I knew I got on her nerves with a lot of my bullshit at times.

I was still kinda high and was liking it. I didn't know when Jericka would be home but I figured that I had a while before she came back in. I got up and headed to the kitchen and poured myself a glass of vodka. I threw a couple of ice cubes into the glass and took a sip of the liquid. I felt it burn my throat. It woulda been a lot worse if I hadn't had the ice though.

I loved that my family was still together but I hated what life had become for us. It didn't make no sense. When I was younger my mother used to tell me that God has a way of humbling you if you don't do it yourself. I knew that shit was true more than ever now because of how far I'd fallen. Jericka had kept shit together for a long time and she was still doing it too. She'd taken the little money that she had saved up and used it to get us this piece of shit two bedroom. Don't get me wrong, Jericka had hooked the place up as much as she could, but, it would never compare to our condo we had.

I needed to get my shit together and I planned on doing it too. I walked back into the living room and sat on the couch. I turned the TV on and flipped through the channels. When I didn't find anything I wanted to watch, I just threw on Training Day cause it was on Netflix. It was one of my favorite movies.

I'd tried to make it clear to Jericka before that I was gonna get my shit together but it didn't seem like she wanted to listen to me. I hated that shit. She was always blowing shit out of proportion and making it seem like I was more far gone than she thought. Yeah, I'd been to rehab a couple of times and shit but it didn't mean nothing. I wasn't one of those people who really liked talking about their feelings like that. I wasn't about to go to rehab and open up to strangers and shit. I also wasn't trying to sit there and let some doctor tell me how I needed to quit. I was young still and I knew that whenever I finally wanted to, I could stop. That time was coming soon enough.

I was gonna be back on top of the world soon enough. I headed into the bedroom and rummaged through the drawer until I found what I was looking for. I went back into the kitchen and made myself another drink before I sat down and got ready to get high again.

After a few more minutes and a couple more sniffs, I was back on cloud nine. I sat there watching Training Day and felt like I was living it out myself. I loved the way that Denzel was a boss. That was gonna be me again one day. I knew that she didn't think it, but I had a plan that Jericka didn't know about. I was planning on getting myself some more drugs, enough for me to sell and still have enough to get high on. I was gonna rebuild my empire and get my shit back together.

People don't know what it's like to have people not believe in you anymore. Whenever I looked at Jericka, I felt bad. I could see in her eyes that I was stressing her out. I just needed her to hold it down for a little longer so I could get my shit all the way together.

I took a deep breath and laid myself out on

the couch. The movie was about to go off. It was at the part where Denzel was about to get killed. I wasn't trying to go out like him though. Once I get back on top, I'm staying there. That thought went through my head as I drifted off back to sleep.

CHAPTER 3

Jericka

I was happy that I had a car and could take myself to and from work. I carried a blade around for protection but I'd never had to use it before. The security at the club was good with the people who worked there. Their last job at the end of the night was to make sure that we got to our means of transportation. Some girls took cabs but I wasn't trying to waste my money by doing that too often.

I liked the drive home because it gave me something that I didn't really get too often which was peace. When I was at work, I was Candace and I needed to be ready for the next person to come and buy my time or else I was on stage dancing. When I was at home I was either the more or the wifey. I took care of Jasheem, making sure he had everything he needed and stuff too. I looked forward to a year in the future when he was six and old enough to start school. Maybe then I'd be able to quit stripping and just work during the day when he was at school.

I didn't know how that was going to happen, not when I still had Hov to deal with. Don't get me wrong, I loved him. We'd been through more shit than a lot of people and we'd come out of it on top and together. When he was good, I was his first lady. Hov made sure that I was always decked out in the flyest shit possible. Bitches on the street couldn't fuck with me. I was the flyest of them all and made sure that as soon as the latest of whatever hit the street, I had it and so did Hov. I played my position.

Now it felt like I was scrambling. I was trying hard to make sure that we could keep our heads above water. As time was going on though, I was starting to see that Hov was becoming more and more of a burden to me and even Jasheem. I loved him and wanted to be with him but I couldn't pretend that he hadn't changed who he was as a person. The physical abuse, spending all the money I gave him on drugs, all of it. I was trying to hold Hov down because he'd been there for me for years when I needed it but he had to wake up and see that shit with us was going in a bad direction and needed to change.

I got home a little after four in the morning. It was still dark as hell outside as I pulled into my parking spot outside of our apartment complex. Before I got out of the car I looked around, making sure no one was out there. Years of being around Hov and his business had made me a little bit more cautious. You never knew when someone was waiting to catch you slipping.

I walked up the little flight of stairs and headed into our apartment. *I told Hov about leaving the TV on when he knew he was gonna fall asleep,* I thought to myself. The TV was the first thing I heard when I came into the house. I dropped my keys on the shelf by the front door and walked into the living room.

Hov was either sleeping, or passed out on the couch. I picked up the remote and turned the TV off. I looked at Hov, noticing how cute he looked when he was sleeping. I took his sneakers off of his feet and dropped them onto the floor in front of him. He didn't even move. I had to look at his stomach to make sure he was still breathing. One of my biggest fears was that I'd come home and find him dead of an over-dose or something like that.

I was glad that he didn't wake up. I knew if he'd gotten up he either would have wanted sex or to argue or to ask about the money I'd made that night. I was tired as hell and didn't feel like being bothered. I wouldn't even be able to get too much sleep because I needed to go to my mother's house. She watched Jasheem for me at nights. It was way too much for me to leave him at home with Hov, even though he didn't have a job. Now that he was on the other side of the product, Hov hung out with some shady people and I wasn't about to let my baby be around that stuff at all.

I turned around and headed into the bedroom quietly. I closed the door behind me and took off my clothes before I climbed into the big bed. I fell asleep quickly and after what seemed like only a few minutes, I was up again.

My mother needed to be at work by 9:30 so I needed to be at her house by 9 at the latest. I was really appreciative of her for looking out for him. She worked all day and had him at night times.

I got to her house right on time. My mother was the hardest working woman I knew. I'd watched her over the years, seeing her struggle but never really letting it break her down. My father had died of a very suddenly heart attack when my brother and I were young so my mom did everything she could to keep a roof over our heads and clothes on our backs. My brother Jayson and I tried not to give her too many problems as we grew up. We fucked up in the way that most normal kids did but nothing too crazy.

I used my key and walked into the house. I didn't have to guess where she or Jasheem were. I followed my nose and ears to the kitchen where she was cooking pancakes and bacon.

"Good morning ma," I said. I walked over to her and kissed her on the cheek.

"Morning baby," she said. I walked over to the chair that Jasheem was sitting in and kissed him on the forehead. "Hi baby boy. How'd you sleep?"

"Good," he said. He wasn't really paying me much attention though. He had an iPad in front of him and was mindlessly eating some of his pancakes and bacon without breaking eye contact with the screen. I laughed. My little boy was something else. He was only 5 but he was smart. Jasheem and I were close. My mother suggested that I put him into daycare or something when he was younger but I told her that since I wasn't working, I didn't mind spending the time with him all day. I'd spent time over the years teaching Jasheem little things. Once he got to school the next year, I just knew that he'd get good grades cause he was already so far advanced.

"How you feeling?" My mother asked. I looked my mother up and down. She was dressed in a black pantsuit that hugged her curves. My mother was like me except that she had a little more weight than I did. She was shorter than me, only 5'2". She has a thick, coke bottle shaped body. She didn't work out but she remained active enough for her to maintain a figure. Her skin and eyes were just like mine.

She had a jet-black weave with a bang in the front that made her look a lot younger. Not to mention that my mother didn't look like the shit she'd been through and she'd been through some shit.

"I'm alright, just tired," I said. I yawned. I was ready to go home and take a nap but that wouldn't be the case.

"I can imagine," she said. My mother and I had a kind of a silent understanding. She didn't mention me stripping and I didn't argue with her about shit for the most part. I loved my mother but she had her own opinions about Hov and our situation. She loved that I was a ride or die type of girl but she hated it too. She told me that she wished that I'd just leave Hov and focus on me.

"You ready for work?" I asked. I made myself a plate of food and sat down next to my son. "Where's Jayson?" My mother and Jayson worked together at a department store in the city. My mother had worked there for years. She made good money from what she said. It was a lot of commission work but she liked it. She became a manager and was making a good salary and every now and then she'd sell something and make a little something extra.

"Jayson's already there," she said. "He took an early shift. You know I had to write him up for being late, right? Damn general manager at my job made me do it just to make sure I would. They must not know that I don't play nice."

"Ma, be nice, don't mess with nobody," I said with a smirk. My mother was small in height but what she lacked there, she made up for in her fierceness. My mother wasn't nothing to be played with at all. She knew how to cut you down with words and once or twice I'd seen her fight and she wasn't nothing to play with when it came to that either.

"I don't mess with nobody unless they mess with me," she said with a smile. "And them making me right up my only son was them messing with me. I don't play like that."

My mother loved Jayson and I with all her heart. After our father died when we were really young, my mother made sure she did what she had to do in order to take care of us. Growing up, we never really had to ask for anything. We didn't have top of the line stuff but we always had enough for us to get by. After I moved out, mommy and Jayson clashed a little bit, but that was only because I wasn't there to be the buffer between them. They got over it though. Jayson was way too overprotective of me and my mother but I think it was cause he was the only boy. He felt the need to be the man of the house and for our family. I appreciated him for that.

"Are you gonna eat?" I asked.

"I already had something," she said. "Besides, I need to be leaving soon anyway."

"Thanks for watching him ma," I said. I reached into my purse and pulled out a $20 bill and handed it to her. She never asked for money but I tried to throw her some money for watching Jasheem whenever I could.

"No problem," she said. "I'll see you guys later. Make sure to lock the door."

"I will," I said.

We finished breakfast and then we headed out. I stopped by the supermarket to pick up a couple of things before we went home. I know a lot of people hated bringing their kids with them places but Jasheem was very well behaved. I loved that about him.

We headed back home and I started getting the few bags out the backseat of the car.

"Mommy, can I help?" Jasheem asked. He was my little helper. He was always offering to help me with something. I could have easily taken the bags in by myself but I let him help, giving him a bag with bread and paper towels inside of it.

"You're my big helper," I said to him as we walked to the apartment. He looked so pleased with himself.

I opened the door to the apartment and could hear the TV was on again. It must have meant that Hov had finally woken up. He came around the corner when he heard the door open. He walked up to me and before he could get all the way to me I could smell the stench of liquor coming off of him. He leaned into my area and kissed me on the cheek and grabbed my ass. I looked at the living room. It looked like Hov had made a halfway attempt to clean up and then stopped halfway through it.

"Wassup baby?" he asked me. He smiled at me. I could see the glossed over look in his eyes but I decided not to try and call him out on it. It didn't make any sense to do it because I wasn't trying to start an argument so damn early in the morning.

"Good morning," I said. I smiled weakly at him.

"Wassup little man?" he asked. He leaned down and scooped Jasheem in his arms. Hov was a good father and I know that he had good intentions at times but he did fuck up. I hated for Jasheem to see him like that. He brought him close to him and kissed him on the cheek. Jasheem's little nose wrinkled and I was sure that he could smell the same thing I was smelling. I doubt that Hov had eaten any breakfast but he was sure powering through some alcohol.

"Jasheem, go put the bag in the kitchen for mommy and then go to your room and pick up your toys," I said.

"OK mommy," he said. He walked down the hall to the kitchen. Hov looked at me and I just walked down the hall to the kitchen to put the rest of the groceries away. I knew that he would be following me in a few minutes.

CHAPTER 4

Hov

I'd woken up early that morning. I didn't know what time it was. I looked at my cell phone and saw that it was about 9:30. I was still tired. I didn't hear anyone in the house which meant that Jericka hadn't come back from getting Jasheem yet.

I got up and made me a little breakfast for myself before I tried to clean up a little bit. I wasn't really good with stuff like that so I quit halfway through it. I turned the TV on and made myself a little drink. Fuck it, it was five o'clock somewhere, right?

Jericka came in a little while later with

Jasheem. It was good that they'd gone food shopping. I'd used up the last of the juice mixing it into my drink.

I watched Jericka as she walked down the hall to the kitchen. She looked good, even though she didn't have on anything special. She looked like she was going to work out in a pair of tight fitting gray sweatpants with a white tank top and gray hoodie. I watched her ass jiggle as she walked down the hall. I wanted some of that but it would have to wait. I had other things on my mind.

I walked into the kitchen soon behind her. Jasheem had already gone to his room. She was moving around putting stuff into cabinets and opening and closing the fridge.

"How is your mother doing?" I asked her. She didn't stop moving as I talked. She knew that I was leading up to something else but I wanted to play it nice. I really liked Jericka's mother. Ms. Lydia was a nice older woman who didn't give me a hard time. When things were good, I made sure that she was well taken care of. She didn't really use the money I gave her but I was sure that she was stashing it for a rainy day or something.

"She's good. She was headed to work when I was over there," she said.

I nodded my head with interest. "Cool, cool," I said. "So how was work?"

"It was alright. It was a little slow though. Not too many people though," she said as she put the last of the groceries away and turned to look at me. Jericka wasn't no dummy. She had to know what I was about to ask her.

"Oh ok, cool. How much did you make?" She reached into her purse and pulled out a wad of cash and handed it to me.

"That's $150," she said. "It was slow like I said, especially for a Thursday."

"Thank you," I said. I took the money and put it into my wallet. I leaned in and kissed her on the cheek.

"No problem," she said.

"So look, I know you think I'm probably gonna go out and spend this money all on shit or whatever but I got a plan. I'm gonna take half of it and spend it on shit to sell. I'm gonna get back on top," I said to her. I smiled at her. She half smiled at me. "I'm trying to make some extra money on the side."

"Anything helps," she said. "I'm about to go

lay down for a little bit. I hope it works out boo."

"It's gonna be fine," I told her.

I left the kitchen and headed into the living room. I could feel the familiar clenching in my jaw. A nigga was ready to get high and soon. I called up my usual guy.

"Yo?" He answered the phone. I'd been getting my drugs from the same nigga for as long as possible. His name was JC. He was this cool Dominican and black dude from the south side. He was one of those people who tried to have their hands in pretty much everything. I liked getting my shit from him because the product was good but more than that, he was discreet. Like I said, I didn't need my business out on the streets and he was usually good about meeting me so that I didn't have to travel to all kinds of places to get what I needed.

"Wassup my guy?" I greeted him. "I'm tryin' to come through and get something."

"Cool," he said, his deep voice filling up my ear. "How much you getting?"

I thought about it for a minute. She'd just given me $150. I could just spend all of it on drugs and sell half of whatever I bought. I thought about it though. It'd be smarter for me to hold some of it. "I got $100 for you."

"Cool, high roller," he said with a chuckle. "You comin' from home?"

"Yeah," I replied.

"Cool," he said. "See you in like 10 or 15 minutes."

"Aight," I said before I hung up the phone.

I walked to the front door and grabbed my car keys. I got in my car and drove for about 10 minutes to a house not too far away. Jericka and I had separate cars. Back in the day when shit was good with us we had a choice of top of the line cars. Now we each had these old ass used cars. I hated it but it was cool to at least have a car.

I got my shit from JC and was trying to act all cool and shit afterwards but I really wanted to get high. I didn't like to be too high around Jasheem. I thought about hittin' up James and seeing what he was up to but I knew that if I did that, he'd want me to smoke him out and I wasn't about to do that. I was really trying to stick to what I said and just only smoke half of it.

"Fuck it," I said. I was driving back to my

house but I decided to just stop and get high. I pulled into an alley that I'd used before. It was behind an abandoned house and next to this field that was filled with garbage. Chicago was so nice in some places and could really be trash in others. It didn't make any sense.

I pulled into the alley and turned the car off. I opened the little baggies that I had and got out a lighter. I pulled out the little glass pipe and got it all set up. I held that shit in my hand and was staring at it. I felt the clenching in the back of my jaw. My mouth started to water and I knew that it was time for me to get high.

I lit that shit, inhaled it and breathed in really deep. I let the smoke fill up my lungs. I started moving in slow motion before I took the next hit.

I rolled down the window. There was a breeze outside and it was coming in. I felt it all over my skin. It felt like it was tingling all over me. I needed to go home. I just wanted to take a nap. I put the car in drive and drove off.

You know how people who are good drivers sometimes say that if they drink or get high or something that it doesn't really affect their driving? I was one of those people. I knew it was stupid to keep doing it but shit had never really gone wrong with it. I guess that there was a limit to that shit though. In my high state, I missed a stop sign and that was the last thing I remembered.

CHAPTER 5

Jericka

I knew that I'd told Hov that I was about to go lay down and I wanted to but I had other stuff to do. It was still early but I decided to just go ahead and make lunch for Jasheem and I. It wasn't anything fancy. I made myself a turkey burger and made him some mini turkey meatballs and French fries. It was one of his favorite things to eat so I made sure that it was healthy, so I used turkey instead of beef or something.

I headed into the living room and actually cleaned up. Hov had half attempted it but I needed to make it all the way clean. Whenever he came back in, he'd probably pass out on the couch again or something but I wanted it to be clean for me.

By the time I finished all of my chores and the food, I was ready for a nap. I grabbed Jasheem and we headed into my room to lay down.

"Are you full boo?" I asked him. He was laying in the bed next to me with his little hand over his stomach.

"I'm sleepy mommy," he said. I laughed at him. His ass had sped through eating the food.

He laid in the bed next to me and snuggled up to me, laying his head on his chest. Jasheem started talking to me about something that happened while he was playing with a neighbor's kid at my mother's house but after a while he drifted off to sleep and so did I after kissing him on the forehead.

I didn't know how long I was sleeping for but it was some good, deep sleep. When the phone started to ring I thought it was happening in my dream. I was dreaming that someone was coming to give me some money and take me out the strip club but I wasn't planning on that happening in real life. My cell phone kept ringing until I finally woke up to answer it.

Jasheem had moved himself from my chest and his feet were somehow in my face. He had his little hand on his chest. My baby was so cute.

I looked at the phone and didn't recognize the number. I picked it up a little too late because it stopped ringing. I was surprised that it started to ring again.

"Hello?" I answered. I cleared my throat and spoke again. I sounded sleepy as hell. "Hello?" I had more clarity in my voice then.

"Hello, is this Jericka Conner?" came the female voice on the other end of the phone.

"Yes, this is she. May I ask who's calling?" I was mad annoyed because it sounded like I'd been woken up from my nap by a fucking bill collector and if that was the case, somebody was about to get hung up on.

"Hi, this is Chicago County Hospital calling," she said. "Do you know a Jehovah Gardner?"

I was confused. I sat up in bed and my heart started to beat a little faster. Why the hell would the hospital be calling me about Hov? I hoped everything was alright but if the hospital was calling, it meant that it wasn't. All types of thoughts went through my head. Had he over-dosed? Did he get into a fight? Was he even alive? I needed answers.

"Yes, yes I know him," I said. "Is everything alright? What happened?" I was trying to be calm but I needed some fuckin' answers. Quickly.

"Ma'am, I'm sorry but I'm unable to give you information over the phone. I can say that he is present here in the hospital. He's a patient here in the emergency room. He is currently being treated and he asked that we give you a call."

"Is he alright? What happened? Why is he in the emergency room?" I needed someone to tell me the truth about whatever was going on.

"Ma'am, he's identified you as his fiancé. I'd love to be able to give your more information over the phone but I can't do that. Please come in as soon as possible and one of the doctors will be able to speak with you. I must also let you know that he's under police supervision currently as he will be arrested when he's done recuperating," she said. She said everything like it was just matter of fact and nothing crazy. I knew she must have made calls like these all the time but I didn't care. I needed some answers. I took down some information from her about where I should go once I got to the hospital and then I got up and started making moves.

I hated waking Jasheem up when he was sleeping but I needed him to get up. I also knew that it would take a few minutes to even get him up because he was a heavy sleeper.

"Jasheem, get up. We gotta go," I said. I nudged him and tried to catch him up but he looked like hell. My poor baby wouldn't be able to make it with me to the hospital. I was fine with that. I didn't know what to do with him.

"Jericka, relax," I said out loud. I needed to just chill the hell out. I needed to get to the hospital but it looked like things were better off than I thought. Hov was obviously awake since he'd given them my number. I didn't know why the police were involved but I needed to get there and see what was going on. I scrolled through my call log and called my best friend, Tamika.

My girl Tamika and I had been best friends since we were in high school. We'd met during our junior year. We were both trying to get on the step team. We'd met during the tryouts and ended up connecting with one another because we were both making fun of the captain, this overweight gay boy with way too much attitude.

We kicked it and she's been my homegirl ever since. I never had to question her loyalty. She had my back like no one else. She was the sister that I'd never had. When Hov took my virginity, she was the first person I called.

I hoped that she was home. Tamika was busy, having her own job and stuff. She was a home health care aide and my girl knew her way around a comb so she did hair on the side too. I admired her though because I'd seen her do shit over the years that made me proud. She was a stripper a couple of years ago and she was the one who suggested I get into it. She'd made a lot of money and saved it so that she could afford to pay to go back to school for her medical certificate. She'd made her money because my girl was bad.

Tamika was light skinned, the color of a coffee with a lot of milk in it. Around her nose she had freckles that she embraced. She had eyes that were naturally light brown. On top she had small breasts but below her waist, she was thick. Thick thighs led to her fat ass. She was a really pretty girl but she was humble about her shit which I loved too. I couldn't stand stuck up people.

Tamika picked up after a couple of rings.

"Hey sis, what's going on?" She answered the phone. She sounded like she was walking somewhere.

"Girl, are you busy?" I asked. I was trying to sound calm but it wasn't easy.

"Nah, not really. I was about to head home. I just finished doing this weave for Ray's girl-friend, Hazel. You alright? Everything good?" She asked.

Tamika was the type who paid attention to everything so it made sense that she'd be able to pick up on when shit wasn't going right with me. I sniffled a little bit as I tried to keep my emotions in check. "Girl, I don't know what's going on," I said.

"What is it? Is it Hov? What did his ass do now?" she asked. She sounded kind of annoyed. When it came to Hov she tried to be supportive but I knew that it wasn't too easy for her cause I told her just about everything when it came to him and how he was.

"Yeah but not how you think," I said. "The hospital just called me telling me that I need to come in. Hov is a patient there and he gave them my number to call me. He's under arrest."

"What?" she asked. She sounded just as surprised as I did. "What the hell is going on?"

"I wish I knew," I said. "Look, if you're not busy can you watch Jasheem for me? My mother is at work and I need to go to the hospital. I gotta figure out what's going on with him."

"Yeah, no problem," she said. I felt a sense of relief wash over me. Tamika had my back for real. "Bring him over when you want. I should be home in like ten minutes. I'll put on a movie and watch it with my godbaby."

"Thank you so much T," I said. "I really appreciate it. I'm gonna get him up now and when I leave the house I'll let you know. I don't know how long I'll be at the hospital but once I get this shit figured out I'll call you and tell you what happened."

"Alright, see you in a few," she said.

"Ok."

I got Jasheem up, even though his little butt wasn't trying to move or do anything. I got him dressed and put him in the car seat of my car.

We got to Tamika's house in like 15 minutes. She came outside to the car to greet us.

"How you doing?" she asked me. She was dressed very simply in a pair of gray sweatpants and a white tank top.

"I'm alright," I said. "I just need to figure out what the hell is going on. And then all this shit with the police being involved too. I wonder what the hell he's done now."

"I know," she said. "Once you figure it out let me know. I'm here for you sis."

"Thanks," I said. I got out of the car and went to the backseat. I grabbed Jasheem and walked him around the car to Tamika. I kneeled down in front of him. "Baby, I have to go take care or something. You're gonna stay with Aunty Tamika for a little bit."

"How long will you be gone?" he asked me. Jasheem wasn't the crying or whining type but he did love his mama and he wanted to be with me as often as he could.

"Not too long boo," I said. I kissed him on the forehead and the cheek and then the lips. "Now, can you be a big boy for me?" I smiled at him.

"Yeah," he said. He smiled back at me.

"Come on boy. Say bye to mommy and let's go watch a movie," Tamika said. She was always good with Jasheem, even though she didn't have any kids of her own. Tamika took his hand and waved bye to me and I watched them walk back into her house.

I was trying to be as cautious as possible while I was driving to the hospital but all the thoughts I had flowing through my head were making me speed up. I needed to know what had happened with Hov.

I ended up driving so fast that I got to the hospital a lot quicker than I thought I would. I parked in the garage under the building and headed inside. I asked the security guard at the front desk where the emergency room was and sped off towards it. I got there and started talking to the lady at the front desk.

"Hi, I got a call about my fiancé, Jehovah Gardner," I said. "He's a patient in your emergency room."

The older woman behind the counter typed some stuff into the computer and told me where to go. "Go down the hall and turn the corner on the right. He's in room 203," she said.

I damn near ran down the hallway. I turned

the door and was surprised to see a police officer outside of his room.

"I'm here to see Hov...I mean Jehovah," I said to the cop. "I'm his fiancé."

"No problem ma'am," he said. "I have to let you know that he's under arrest."

"Ok," I said. I didn't like cops. I tried to avoid them as much as possible. Years of being with Hov had made me naturally cautious.

I walked into the room and felt the tears start. Hov was laying on the bed with his eyes closed. My baby looked bad. He was hooked up to and IV. He was bruised all over and had a couple of bandages all over his body. He had a cut on his leg that was bleeding through the bandage.

I walked over to him and sat on the edge of the bed. "Hov?" I said it softly. I didn't know if he was sleeping or what so I wasn't trying to bother him too much.

"Jericka?" He opened his eyes and looked at me. He sat up slowly and leaned back in the bed. With every movement he moaned and groaned. He was in so much pain. Hov wasn't the emotional type at all but he broke down crying.

He grabbed me with his free hand. His other arm was handcuffed to the bed. He reached out and pulled me in for a hug. I hugged him back, trying not to hurt him. We sat there for over a minute just holding on to one another and letting the tears flow. Hov and I had a bond. He was like my heart. He wasn't perfect at all but he and I had made it work for such a long time that we just clicked.

"Hov, what happened?" I asked. I pulled back from him. I was staring at him in his eyes, not taking my eyes off of his.

"Baby I don't know," he said. "I was in a car accident. It was bad. I think I blacked out when I was high or something. I think I passed out at the wheel." He wiped his eyes. I

I shook my head at him. "Hov, I want you to listen to me," I said. I made sure I was looking at him right in his eyes. He needed to know that I was serious about what I was about to say. "You need to stop the shit. All of it. I'm not even talking about how shit used to be. We can get back on top but the only way for us to do it is if you get clean and stay clean. You can't be out here fucking up like this. Now you got the cops involved and shit. I can't believe this." I paused because I needed to gather my emotions.

"Don't you care about your family?" I asked. "Don't you care about us more than you care about the drugs and shit? You gotta be clean baby. You gots to. Ain't no way that you gonna survive out here. I be trying to act like I don't notice it but you're doing worse. You use me. You use all types of shit now. I don't wanna have to tell our son that his father died cause he was too weak to beat his addiction."

Hov was looking at me and the look in his eyes was telling me that he was listening to what I was saying. I hoped that it was true. I hoped Hov had listened to everything that I'd just said and was taking it to heart. I meant every single word of it. I wanted him to be clean, not just for me or Jah, but for him too. I really did believe that unless he changed shit around, he was going to die. Hopefully he didn't take anyone down with him.

"Jericka, I promise I'm gonna get clean," he said. "I mean it."

"From your mouth to God's ears," I said. I grabbed him again in a hug and we started crying again.

CHAPTER 6

Hov

I sat across from Jericka, feeling all broken and shit. I loved her and knew I could be vulnerable with her but I'd never been the crying type. I think a lot of it was seeing her cry. Jericka wasn't like other chicks. She was a lot stronger than other people I knew, men included. I knew that if she was crying it meant that she'd hit rock bottom.

I'd hit rock bottom myself. How the fuck did I let my shit get this bad? I needed to really just sit and realize that I was there because of shit that I'd done. Instead of taking care of him, I was out getting drugs and getting high. I felt fucked up about it because it was really my own doing. No one had put me into this position but me. I hated seeing her cry like that. It really hurt me to my core to watch my baby with those tears streaming down her face. The thoughts going through my mind were about Jericka and Jasheem and how I just wanted for shit to be better for them.

"Jericka, the cops are saying I'm under arrest as soon as I'm good enough to get out of here," he said. "I'm not trying to be in no fuckin' lock up. I wanna be home with you and Jah."

"Baby, what are you under arrest for? What do you remember?" Jericka asked.

I took a deep breath and sighed loudly. "Well like I said, I linked with JC and got some shit from him, just like I planned to. I stopped in an alley and got high." I paused. She looked annoyed with me but she didn't try and interrupt me. "So after that I was driving home. I remember not stopping at a stop sign and then the next thing I knew, I woke up in the back of an ambulance." I paused as I thought about what they'd told me when I woke up.

"When I woke up, I didn't know what the

fuck was going on," I said. "I had on a neck brace and I felt like I'd gotten the shit kicked out of me all over my damn body. They told me that I'd been in a car accident." I had to pause to try and keep my emotions together. "They said that I hit another car. They said that I'd crashed into a woman and her kid."

"Oh God, Hov," Jericka cried. She covered her mouth and kept on crying.

"I know," I said. I looked down at the ground. I was feeling real sorry for myself right then.

"What happened to them?" She asked. She looked like she was afraid to even ask the question.

"They're both here," I said. I looked into her eyes again. "I asked about them and they're both in surgery. The doctors said they're both in surgery for different shit. It could go either way."

Jericka stood up and turned away from me. I knew my baby had to be going through it right then. She'd been there to support me through everything I'd been through but this a whole other thing. I'd done my dirt in the streets. I'd busted shots when it came down to it cause I wasn't pussy. I'd never been in a situation like that one though. A mother and her child could die cause of me and my need to do drugs. That shit didn't sit right with me at all.

"Jericka...I..." I was trying to come up with the right thing to say but I couldn't find the words. "Baby I'm sorry."

"What are the cops saying?" she asked me.

"What?"

"What are the cops saying?"

"I'm not even gonna hold you baby, shit don't look too good for your boy," I said. There was no point in beating around the bush. "They still ain't get into everything about it because I'm here and they can't take me nowhere anytime soon. The first cop that came though told me that I'd better be praying for the mother and the kid to make it through surgery. I had drugs on me and I was high. Shit's looking crazy right now."

"What a fucking shame," she said. "I can't believe this, Hov. How could you fuck up like this? Did you even think before you did that shit?" She paused and I knew she was trying to

get her feelings together but I deserved everything that she was throwing at me. "Hov, what if
that was me and Jasheem? I know that you think
that this little addiction isn't a problem but it is.
Doing what you did in the streets was one thing
but now look at you. This is real. I don't know if
I can be with you through this. You fucked up
real bad and it's nothing I can do to help you. I
hate this feeling."

That shit hurt my heart. Jericka had been
there with me through thick and thin. We didn't
have stories; we had books. Our shit was deep so
I knew that if she was saying that she didn't
know if she'd be able to stick by me, she meant
it. I wouldn't be able to deal with that shit at all.
"Jericka, you think I don't know that? I'm
sorry," I said. "If I get a chance I wanna apologize to that lady and her kid. I can't do this shit
without you though. I'm dead ass. The only way
that shit is gonna get better for us is with you
and Jasheem by my side. I need my family
Jericka. I'd die without y'all. If you and Jasheem
leave me, it's over. I wouldn't give a fuck if I
lived or died after that. What would be the point
of going on if I don't even have my family?"

There was a knock at the door and then the

pig standing outside the door came inside. "Ma'am, you've got 5 more minutes and then you have to go," he said to Jericka.

"Ok," she said. He closed the door and went back outside.

"Jericka," I said. She finally turned back around. She was looking at me in my eyes now. I was staring back because I wanted her to know how serious about this I was. "I'm sorry for all of it. All of it. I'm gonna get clean. I promise you that. I'm not gonna keep fucking around. You think I wanna lose all I got left?" I wanted Jericka to know that I was serious as hell about what I was saying. I was a hood dude but it wasn't like I didn't have a heart. I needed them by my side if shit was ever gonna get better for us.

"I believe you," Jericka said. The cop came and knocked on the door letting us know that it was time for Jericka to leave. She came over to me and kissed me on the lips for a couple of seconds. I felt that shit for real. I knew she probably had a lot of shit that she wanted to say but it was cool cause I knew she'd be there for me so we'd have all the time in the world to hear it.

"See you at my hearing," I said to Jericka as

she walked out of the room, leaving me alone
with my thoughts.

CHAPTER 7

Jericka

With everything going on with Hov, the last place I wanted to be was also the same place I needed to be: the strip club. I was debating back and forth about it, wondering if it would be in my best interest to go. Tamika had convinced me that I should go. She said that if I did plan on bailing Hov out of jail that I should have the money to do it. I thought about it and realized that she was right. I was the only person who'd be able to help him out of jail. I needed to take my ass to work so that was exactly what I did.

My mind was all over the place and I just

wanted that shit to calm the fuck down. I needed to be clear headed but it wasn't working out for me. I wanted to focus on one thing—anything at that point—but I couldn't. All these thoughts were running through my head like it was a race track or something and I didn't know what the hell to do about them. I was hoping that everything with Hov was gonna be alright. I wanted my man home, not in the hospital and definitely not in jail. I still couldn't believe that he'd fucked up the way that he did. It was bad enough to get caught with the drugs but then to be caught high and almost kill someone? His ass would be lucky if they didn't put him *under* the jail. I was upset with myself too. I felt like I was enabling him or something by bailing his ass out again, but what was my alternative?

The worst part about the night was that I didn't really have anyone to talk to about it with. Don't get me wrong, a couple of the bitches that worked with me at the club were cool, but I wasn't friends with *any* of them. We worked in a business where the next bitch would gladly take from you without a care. The girls that I was cool with did shit fair for the most, but I had to check too many of these girls too many times for me to feel comfortable. I'd been there for almost two years now though so they knew that if they stayed out of my way that I'd stay out of theirs too.

I was just in a bad mood that night. The thing about the strip club was that you had to be a salesperson. You had to get up on stage or in a booth and sell these niggas a fantasy and shit. You had to make them believe that you were theirs and that even if they were clearly unattractive and stuff that they still had a chance with you. I didn't feel like acting all happy and shit. I wanted to just sit in my own house and get my thoughts together but I couldn't do that cause like always, it was up to me to fix stuff.

I was in the dressing room finishing my makeup and stuff. I was naturally pretty but like I said, I had to sell a dream. My makeup, long weave, and my outfit were all a part of that.

My phone started to vibrate. I saw that it was Tamika calling me. My shift hadn't started yet so I had a couple of minutes to talk to her. I sat down in the chair in front of the vanity mirror and picked it up.

"Hey Mika," I answered the phone.

"Wassup Jericka? You at work?" she asked.

"You know it," I said. "You made sense earlier. I gotta make the money to bail out Hov. I got a good feeling about tonight." I didn't know what it was but I felt like by the end of the night that I'd be happy to have come into work.

"I'm glad you got a good feeling," she said. "Although if you ask me, you could just leave Hov in jail for a little bit. That's a grown ass man and he can take care of himself, but that's none of my business."

"Don't start," I said. Tamika liked Hov when we first got together. She even dated one of his friends for a while before he got some other girl pregnant. Once Hov started doing drugs, Tamika told me that I should leave him. She said that it didn't make any sense for me to stress myself out over him, especially when he didn't care enough about himself not to do drugs. Once I told her that that he hit me, that was it. She was ready to call her brother and boyfriend at the time and have them jump him. I had to talk her down from doing that. It wasn't that she disliked him though. Tamika was just super protective over me because we'd been friends for so long. It worked both ways though.

"I won't," she said. "So what's on your

mind? I mean...I know what's on your mind but I want you to say it."

I sat back in the chair. Most of the other girls were upstairs except for two of them on the other side of the room. I wasn't a fan of talking about Hov at work. I was sure that a lot of these bitches already knew the story of him and shit. I didn't wanna give them any more information for them to run back and tell other people. "This shit with Hov is stressing me the fuck out," I said. "Like...I really can't get him off my mind."

"And how do you feel about it?" Tamika had read a couple of books and binge watched Iyanla and shit and all of a sudden she was a psychiatrist. It was cool though; I needed someone to talk to and she was the only one.

"Girl, I'm embarrassed," I admitted to her. "I really am. I can't believe he did this. I feel like I look stupid staying with him sometimes." I hated to admit that out loud but I had to be honest. "Hov almost killed a mother and a child. Do you know how that shit makes me feel? I'm so sorry for them but how do I look trying to go apologize when I'm the reason he got high? He got the money from me."

I had to pause. I was getting a little emotional just thinking about it all over again. I looked around and no one was paying me any attention at all.

"I'm just tired," I said with a sigh. I took a deep breath. "I want to drop Jasheem off at my mother's house and I couldn't even tell her what was going on. She knew something was up but I didn't have the heart to mention anything about it to her. You know I tell my mother everything."

"Wow girl," said Tamika. "That's crazy. You know how close you and Ms. Lydia are. You tell her everything."

"I know," I said sadly. "Oh well. Ain't nothing to do about it now. I already told Hov that I'd be there when he goes to court. I can't just leave him alone. He needs me."

"You also need you," she said.

"I got me. I know you do to," I told her.

"That's right," Tamika said.

"Aright girl, let me finish this makeup and take me ass out here," I said.

"Alright sis, call me later. I'll be up for a while. I got a late-night client coming through," she said.

"Who's coming through to get their hair done this late?" I asked. It was almost midnight.

Tamika busted out laughing. "Girl, it's a client but it ain't for no hair," she said with a laugh.

"Yessss sis, have fun," I said. I started laughing as I hung up the phone. She was about to get her groove on. It felt like it'd been forever since Hov and I had done the do and with him going through what he was going through, I figured it would probably be awhile before we did it again.

I finished putting on my makeup. I always tried to keep it simple with the makeup. I hated piling all that shit on my face. I checked my outfit out in the mirror. I was feeling it tonight so I brought out something a little different. I'd recently bought a two piece all white swimsuit set. I planned on taking it off *very* slowly. I wanted those dudes to make sure they were tipping before they saw anything. I'd purposely gotten the white outfit because I knew how much guys loved seeing it against my cocoa colored skin. I checked myself out in the mirror, making sure I looked good before heading out to the main floor. It was show time.

I liked to get out on the floor a couple of minutes before I hit the stage. I liked to walk around the whole place and just get a feel for it. I had developed the eye. I could spot the ballers and stuff. Plus, we always had a lot of regulars who were there all the time and I wanted to see how many people I might have to get for a lap dance.

I walked out to the floor and started slowly making my way around. The name of the club was Diamonds. It was a nice club too. The stage was in the middle of the club. It was surrounded by the bar where we had a couple of bad bitches bartending. Outside of the bar all around the walls were the tables that people could get bottle service and stuff like that. I walked around the whole club once, making sure my walk was sexy. Of course a couple of guys tried to stop me but I promised I'd come and see them after I got off the stage. Like I said, you had to sell the fantasy.

It was my time to hit the stage. We had an in-house DJ who'd worked at the club for just about as long as I had. His name was Tommy but he was better known to everyone as DJ

Bangers. He had a feel for the shit that we liked to hear.

"Fellas, we got something really special for you tonight. Coming to the stage, dressed in all white cause she's feeling Godly, is Raven!" DJ Bangers announced me. I had gone back stage but I came out when he called my name. I walked passed this other girl, one that that I was cool with. Her name was Chantal. She was this Spanish chick with a fat ass that she swore was real but didn't look like it.

"Good luck," she said. "It's not hittin' for much out there," she said. She held up the small handful of bills that she had in her hand. It didn't look like much, but I already knew that I could do better.

My music came on and I went to work. The way that I got through my time on the stage was really simple. I just acted like there wasn't a whole room full of people staring at me. I pretended that I was doing a sexy ass dance in my mirror at home and not in front of anyone.

I walked down the long stage until I got to the end. I walked up to the pole slowly and wrapped my fingers around it. I started to do my dance. I made my body move to the beat of the music. I bent down in front of the pole and danced into a split. I let my body move and made my ass jiggle up and down in front of them. I heard a couple of people start to make clapping and cheering noises and I knew that I was getting them hooked. Wait till they saw what I had next up.

I wrapped my legs around the pole and threw my head back. My hair flew behind me, touching the lower part of my back. I started making it clap. I turned around and put my back on the pole, letting it get between my cheeks. I started taking off my top to the sound of the music.

The lighting in the club was brighter around the stage area than it was anywhere else. They wanted for us to be seen. I looked out over the crowd and my eyes landed on some dude I hadn't seen before. He was sitting at the bar, sipping on something brown and staring at me.

Now, this was the strip club which meant that niggas stared at me all the time. The thing that was taking me off guard was that he wasn't just staring, he was staring *hard*. It was like he was mesmerized or something. He was looking at me like he was trying to memorize every curve and outline of my body.

He and I made contact and he winked at me. I had to admit that he was handsome too. I couldn't tell how tall he was because he was sitting down and stuff but I could see his face. He was dressed really simple in a plain black V-neck t-shirt. A thick gold chain hung loosely over his chest with a cross at the end of it. He was big as shit, really muscular. He had dreadlocks that hung freely over his face that came down past his shoulders. There was a tattoo on his neck but I couldn't tell what it was of. His skin was the same color as mine and he had these hazel eyes that seemed to catch the light in the club. On top of all of that, he was handsome too. He had smooth skin and a strong jawline. I didn't usually go for the dreadhead type but he was fine as hell.

I kept my dance going and I got more nervous than I usually did. He was staring at me so intently that it almost threw me off. I kept on dancing as my second song came on. People were throwing money and I hadn't even realized. I was so caught up in looking into his eyes that I almost forgot about everyone else.

Whoever he was, he clearly had money. First he started throwing ones but after a while he started throwing bigger bills: fives, tens, and twenties. I kept on dancing all through the song. It was clear that he was interested in me and he definitely had the money to keep my attention. When I was done dancing, I got up to pick up my money. Over my time working at the club I'd figured out how to do a mental count. I definitely had made some good money. All I needed was a couple of dances and stuff and it would be a good night.

I got off the stage and put my money away. One thing I didn't play with was my money. Them other bitches were known to steal so I never took any chances. I always put my money in a safe and secure place where it wasn't gonna be touched.

I headed to the back and changed my outfit. I came back out to the floor with a lime green one piece outfit on. I was walking through the crowd of people trying to find the dreadhead dude. A couple of my regulars tried to stop me and some new people. They must have seen me on the stage. The club was packed more than usual, which was good, but it also made it harder for me to find him. I finally spotted him after a couple of minutes of searching. I walked up to him slowly and almost on cue, he turned around.

He was taller than I would have imagined. He had to be about 6'2" or 6'3". He was also more handsome than I could see from the stage.

"Wassup?" he greeted me. His face was serious but he didn't seem unfriendly or anything like that. His face was straight like he was just calm. It was almost like he was expecting me. "You looking for me?"

"What?" I asked. I was all nervous and shit. I don't know why though. Something about this dude was throwing me off my usual balance.

"I asked was you looking for me?" He said.

"Why would I be doing that?" I asked. I got back some of my usual composure.

"I think you know why," he said. "You tryin' to do a private dance?"

"Sure," I said. He grabbed me by the hand and led me to the back where the private rooms were. He paid the security guard the usual fee and we went to one of the rooms. He ordered a bottle of champagne and popped it when it came.

The two of us were in the small room with one another and I inhaled the fainting fragrance of his cologne. I didn't know what it was but it smelled like heavenly. I peeped the dude, taking him all in. He was very muscular. It looked like he worked out.

"You want a glass?" he asked. Everything about him seemed so cool and collected like he was just so sure of himself. I didn't know who he was but a dude like that could either be a gift or a curse.

"Yeah," I said. He poured me out a glass of champagne. I sipped it quickly and put it down on the ground.

I had to admit to myself that I was mad attracted to that dude. He was turning me on and he wasn't doing shit but sitting in the chair with his hands folded behind his head.

I started to do my dance, moving my hips and ass to the slow, soft music that was playing. I was working my hips back and forth. I took off the top of the one piece and before I knew it, I was butt ass naked. He had pulled out a wad of ones and was letting them drop to the floor like it was rain.

I backed up and sat on his lap. He was kind

of hard and if I was feeling it right, he was working with something big. I grinded my naked ass back and forth on his dick. The air in the room was thick with the sexual tension between us. He was clearly turned on. He quit playing cool and had his hand on my breast. Usually I had a no touching rule but I was willing to let him bend it as long as he didn't try and do too much. Besides, he was tipping like crazy and I needed the money to help Hov.

"Hold up," he said to me out of nowhere. I stopped dancing and turned around to look at him. I was confused. I don't think anyone had stopped me during a dance before.

"Something wrong? You leaving?" I asked.

"Nah, everything's cool," he said in his deep voice. "I just wanna chill. Is that cool?"

"Sure, it's your money," I said with a smirk. "The only thing is that they're gonna ask for me to be back out there soon though."

"Nah they won't," he said. "I paid to chill with you for at least the next two hours and I can pay for longer if I want to."

Yeah, he was a baller for real. He'd had to have put down some serious money for him to pay for my time for that long. "Ok cool," I said.

"Look, I don't know what you had in mind but this ain't one of those places where you can fuck the strippers. Some of them other bitches do that but I'm not one of them."

"Chill," he said. "I wasn't trying to smash or nothin. I just wanted to talk to you. I like the way you move and shit. You carry yourself different than the rest of them. It's something about you that I like."

"Oh word?" I said. I wasn't one of those types who got turned on by money and shit. I loved loyalty. It was for that reason that I had never cheated on Hov and I didn't have any plans to do so either. This new dude, whoever he may be, was mad cool and all but I wasn't about to get hype off of it. I had to admit though that there was definitely something happening between us. I didn't know what it was but he was turning me on for real and I knew that he was feeling me too.

"Yeah," he said. "So just chill, sip on that overpriced champagne and tell me about you."

"What you wanna know?" I asked. I didn't really chat with the clients like that. I preferred to keep it more professional than that but this dude had paid for my time so I was gonna give it to him. Not to mention that something about him just made it seem like he was the easy to talk to type.

"How bout we start off simple?" He asked me. "What's your real name?"

"Hmm," I thought out loud. "I don't usually tell people stuff like that. But my name is Jericka. What about yours?"

"I'm Marco," he said and smiled a little bit. "It's nice to meet you for real, *Jericka.*" He said my name like it was the sexiest thing in the world and I had to admit that I loved the way that he was saying it. I wanted him to say it some more.

"It's nice to meet you too, Marco," I said. I moved and poured myself another glass of the champagne he bought. I was sitting there naked as the day I was born and he wasn't holding back from checking me out. I didn't mind it though. Usually when guys stared at me it was in such a creepy way. Marco was looking at me like I was the big trophy after a basketball game or something.

"So where you from?" he asked me.

"I was born in Atlanta but we moved here to

Chi Town when I was little. It was me, my brother and our mother," I explained.

"Oh word? Southern born, huh? I guess that explains your thickness," he said. He looked me up and down, his eyes resting on my ass. I knew he had to be thinking about what he was could do with it if he had the chance. I almost let myself wonder the same thing.

"Yeah, that's me," I said. "I love Chicago though. I might have been born in Atlanta but my roots are here."

"I feel you," he said. "What you got going on now?"

"What you mean?" he asked me.

"I mean who you stay with now? What's your life like? I'm down to here all that shit," he said. He smirked at me.

I figured out what it was just then that made Marco different from the other clowns that came into the club or even tried to talk to me on the street. It was his charm. I didn't know what it was about him but Marco was charming as hell. I didn't know shit about him but his name but I liked him. The way that he carried himself was just different. He was a boss. I knew that for sure. I just wanted to figure out in what way.

"That's a little personal," I said to him. "Why don't you tell me something about you first?"

"Ah ha," he smiled for the first time. He had these beautifully white teeth that looked amazing.

"What?" I asked

"Nothing," he said. "It's just that you're mad cautious and shit. I like that. You don't know me from Adam."

"Yeah," I said. "Not trying to be rude or anything like that. I just don't wanna sit here chopping it up with one man and talking about the next, at least not yet."

"I feel you," he said. "Well like I said, my name is Marco. I'm from Chicago, born and raised on the Southside. I just got out the joint not too long ago. I did two years."

"For what?" I asked. I was curious.

"Doesn't matter. It was some bullshit but I did that shit on my head," he said. "Now I'm back in town and I gotta fix some shit my brother messed up."

"Oh word? Like what?" I asked.

"I'm sure you'll find out soon enough if your ear is to the streets," he said in a mysterious way.

"But now that I told you something about me, I want you to tell me about you, Jericka." He spoke slowly and deliberately like every word he said was the most important thing in the world. It worked out though cause it made me want to pay attention to him even more.

"I mean...I don't know what to say," I said. I knew that there were lots of things I could say but I didn't know Marco like that.

"Yo," he said, snapping me from my thoughts. "I know you don't know me or shit but I'm just tryin' to get to know you. We don't have to talk about shit that you don't wanna talk about."

"Ok cool," I said.

"How about this?" Marco said. "How about you tell me how you got into this shit? You don't seem like the typical stripper and shit."

"Ok," I said "Well, I've been doing this for like two years."

"You like it?" he asked.

"I mean...it's a job. It pays the bills. It keeps clothes on me and my son's back. Is it what I wanted to do with my life? Hell no. It's just something to keep the roof over our heads until shit gets better," I explained to him.

"I feel you," he said. "I can relate to that. We do what we gotta do to survive. That's like the number one unwritten rule of the streets."

"Word," I said.

"So you got a son, huh? How old is he?" Marco asked.

I smiled just thinking about my baby. "His name is Jasheem. He's five years old. I love him so much," I said.

"That's good," said Marco. "What about his father?"

The smile slowly faded from my face. "What about him?" I asked.

"Is he still in the picture? It sounds like you're struggling right now so I'm assuming he's not," Marco said.

"Yeah, Hov is still around," I said absent-mindedly. "I mean...as around as he can be I guess."

"What does that mean?" he asked.

I sighed loudly. "I mean...I don't even know where to start. Hov and I been together for a long time. He was my first love and stuff. Things with us were good but it all went left a while ago." I paused. I didn't realize how much baggage I was carrying around with me when it came to Hov but it was slowly coming out little by little. "I don't know. I just never thought that we'd get to this point. He used to be the man, running the streets and shit and then…" My voice trailed off.

"And then?" Marco asked. He put his hand on my back in a reassuring way.

"And then Hov made a choice and I've been the one payin' for that shit ever since," I said. I knew I sounded bitter and stuff and I guess I did have a lot of bitterness inside me.

"What choice was that?"

I just started shaking my head. "That nigga put drugs before us…before his family. Hov started doing drugs…and I don't mean weed or anything like that. I mean real hard shit. He was getting high on his own product and that was when shit went left for us. We lost everything we had…money, cars, our home, all of it. Hov's name doesn't mean shit to anyone. But I loved him and we have a family together so I did what I had to do. I started doing this cause it pays the bills."

"I feel you," Marco said. "Survival is key. I mean…I'm not gonna knock you for doing what you did or anything like that. Family is something else sometimes they'll drag you down quicker than an enemy will."

"Yeah, that's true," I said.

"But if that nigga is really strung out on that bullshit like you say he is, you might need to let that nigga go," Marco said.

"I can't leave Hov," I said. "He needs me."

"Yeah he does," Marco said, "but what about you? Who got your back? If you was my shorty you wouldn't want for nothing. I ain't never seen nobody like you before. You're just different, dead ass. You need to stop fuckin with that lame and get with a big-time nigga like me."

I just looked at Marco and didn't know what to say. His confidence was coming off of him in waves like good cologne.

"Look, I gotta go. I got some shit to handle tonight. Here you go," he said. He pulled out a wad of cash and peeled off a crisp $100 bill. He handed it to me. "Take this, and this." He pulled a pen from his pocket and wrote his telephone number on the bill.

"Give me a call when you ready to stop fuckin' with a lame and get with a real nigga. I can help you out, you and your son," said

Marco. He leaned down and kissed me on the cheek before he walked out of the room.

I sat in the room trying to get my thoughts together.

What the fuck was that? I thought to myself.

CHAPTER 8

Hov

After Jericka left, I didn't have anything to do. They hadn't taken me into custody or anything yet but they let me know that I'd be out of the hospital after another night or so. I had nothing to do but sit there and think about shit. They'd taken my phone. They wouldn't even let me have a book or something.

I laid in the bed for hours, only getting up to go to the bathroom. I sat in the chair by the bed and would move back to the bed. I took a nap and woke up later on and the only thing for me to do was to take another nap. I hated being

bored. An idle mind was really the devil's play-
ground. I hoped that Jericka was working on
making some money for my bail hearing...when-
ever that would be. I needed her to just hold me
down this one more time before I got my shit
together. I wasn't in a position to make stuff
better for myself, at least not until I beat this
case and these charges. I hadn't even been
arraigned yet so I didn't know what they'd be
charging me with. I hoped that I got a good
public defender cause I wasn't trying to do any
more time.

The next morning the doctor came into the
room mad early. The clock on the wall said that
it was a little after seven in the morning. I hadn't
even been asleep for too long cause of all the
naps I'd taken the day before. I just wanted to
be out the hospital but I wasn't in any rush at all
to get to the jail.

"Mr. Gardner," came the voice of the short
Indian looking doctor. "How are you feeling?"

"I feel alright, just a little bruised and what
not," I said.

"That's to be expected," he said. "Well,
we've monitored you overnight and you're not

showing any signs of a concussion or anything. We wanted to keep you overnight to make sure but it all checks out. Now, you'll be bruised and in some pain for the next few days but it'll go away. I'm going to make sure that you get some painkillers."

"Thanks doc," I said. He was standing mad far back from me and wasn't making eye contact. He was probably scared of me. That whole big black man shit along with the fact that he probably knew that I was going to jail were probably too much for him. I didn't blame him.

"No problem," he said. "Well, once we get this paperwork all processed, you'll be on your way. The officers will come in and escort you wherever they're taking you. I hope it all works out for you Mr. Gardner."

"Thank you," I said. A thought crossed my mind. "Hey Doc. I have a question."

"Yes, what is it?" he asked. He'd walked back over to the door and was just about to leave.

"When I came in, I hit another car. There was a mother and a kid in it. Are they alright?" I asked.

"I'm sorry, but I can't give you any information about either of their conditions unless
you're family," he said. He tried to leave but I
stopped him.

"Wait," I said. "Please, just...are they still
alive at least? I'm not asking cause of all this
court shit. It's cause I just wanna know for
myself," I said. I was being serious with him. I
didn't want to have to walk around with that on
my conscience too. I knew that I'd fucked up by
getting behind the wheel and being high and in
the long run I'd have to pay for it, whether they
were alright or not. I just wanted to make sure
they were alright.

"Yes, both of them are alive," he said. "I
can't tell you anything else besides that."

"Thank you. I appreciate it," I said to him.
He walked out of the room.

A nurse came in a couple of minutes later
and disconnected me from the IV that I was
hooked up to. After about an hour or so, two
police officers came into the room. They told
me that I needed to get dressed and come with
them. I got dressed slowly. That wasn't my first
time getting arrested so I already knew what to

expect. I didn't wanna go back inside a jail though.

The booking process was annoying as shit. Cops acted like you were a fucked-up person all cause you got arrested. I hated that shit. I was never good at following the rules so all of their different rules didn't sit right with me.

I went through the whole process though. There was the waiting part. We got to the station and I got fingerprinted and photographed. They took me on a bus with a bunch of other people to the county lock up where central booking was. It was mid-afternoon when I got there. They gave me another set of clothes, plain prison shit, and showed me where my cell was.

I sat on the little bunk on the bottom. I looked around the tiny ass room, annoyed with myself for even allowing myself to end up back in there. I had nothing all over again. Nothing except for four walls, a toilet and nothing else. I prayed silently that my bail wasn't gonna be too high because I needed to get the fuck up outta there.

When I was being walked to my cell, I felt the eyes of other people on me. I spotted a couple of dudes I knew, some friends and some enemies. That was the funny thing about jail: at the end of the day you could be the corner store crackhead or a fucking billionaire but it didn't matter cause prison walls didn't discriminate against nobody. The system was rigged against you once you were inside.

I chilled out in my cell for about an hour. A bunch of niggas walked by. They'd slow down to look into my cell as I passed. I knew how that could be. Everyone wanted to see the new dude. It probably also made niggas hype to know that it was me in there. It was crazy how far I'd let myself fall. I used to employ some of these niggas. Some of these other dudes used to be customers and get their product from me.

A while later when it came time for the nightly lockdown the dude who I assumed was my cellmate came inside the cell. He was an older cat. The dude had to be at least 50 years old. He had a short Caesar haircut and a full beard. His hair was salt and pepper colored. He had more than a few tattoos. He looked like he still worked out but his body was getting old.

"Oh shit. I heard about the new dude but I ain't think he was my cellmate," he said. He walked over to me and held out his hand. "What's up young blood? They call me Speedy."

I looked at him and his extended hand. I took a couple of seconds before I shook it. I'd learned over time to be naturally distrustful of people who seemed to be too friendly. I took his hand and shook it firmly.

"Wassup? I'm Hov," I said.

"Oh shit. That's a name that rings bells around here," he said. He climbed up to the top bunk.

"Yeah I guess," I said. Remembering when I was bigger deal was starting to become a painful memory for me. It only reminded me of how far I'd fallen.

"So what you in here for?" He asked me.

"It don't matter," I said. Information was power and I wasn't trying to give that old dude any power over me.

"Oh, you one of those, huh? The strong silent type? Well it's alright. We ain't got nothin' but time and space. It ain't late enough to go to sleep so you'll talk when you wanna," he said.

"We'll see," I said. "What about you?"

"I been in here for a couple of months this

time around young blood," he said. "This time I'm in for robbing someone."

"Oh word? Who?"

"Does it matter? I just saw someone on the street and decided that I needed the money they were flashing. I was on drugs bad...real bad," he said. He climbed down off his bunk and sat on the floor in front of me. His eyes looked so damn sad that it was pitiful.

"What were you on?" I asked.

"Shit...didn't matter. Weed wasn't strong enough for me after a while. I dibble and dabble in what I could get my hands on. I just wanted my next high. So I was walking down the street on the west side, minding my business when I spotted some chick in front of me. She'd just come from the ATM machine and shit so I knew she had cash. I was already high and was coming down so I wanted more money. I grabbed her and pulled her into an alley. I pistol whipped her a couple of times and took all her cash."

"Wow," I said. In some ways, I really did relate to him. I felt like he could have been me or vice versa. I'd never robbed anyone just for money for my shit but I felt like with the way that shit was going, I might not have been too far off. "That's crazy yo. So what these cops saying?"

"It don't even matter. I'm gettin charged with robbery and assault with a deadly weapon. They set my bail and I only have to pay $5000 to get out," he explained.

"So why you still in here?" I asked him. I didn't know how much my bail would be but I knew that if push came to shove, I was sure that Jericka had money saved up. Besides all that, her mother definitely had money saved.

"Ain't got nobody to post the bail," he said sadly. "I'm sitting in here knowing only a few thousand dollars could set me free but also knowing that ain't a bitch coming to pay it for me."

"Why's that?"

"Man, cause that's how life works," he said. Speedy stood up and walked to the door of the cell. He looked out through the bars like he was imagining some shit or something. "You think that was the first time I did some stupid shit when I was high on drugs? Hell nah. I had it all. I had a wife and three kids. You think any of them come and see me? Nah. My wife remarried to some other dude and my kids are grown. I got grandkids I ain't never meet. it's all my fault though. I forgot what was important."

I didn't say anything back cause I just wanted to be quiet for a minute. It was strange the way that shit worked out sometimes. I'd gone to jail for doing some dumb shit involving drugs and now I had a dude in front of me telling me about him doing the same thing. It was like he was a mirror to what my life could be if I didn't end up fixing it the way that it should be.

"I feel you," I said. I took a deep breath. "I mean...I don't think my shit is as bad as that but I got some problems that I gotta fix."

Speedy turned back around to look at me. "Like what? You on that shit too?"

I nodded sadly. "Yeah. But I'm trying to clean up," I said.

"Were you trying to clean up before you ended up in here? Or did it start since you got arrested?" Speedy asked the question but I was sure that he already knew the answer. I don't know what it was about him but that old cat seemed to know some shit.

"It don't matter," I said. "I'm gonna clean up."

"I hope so," he said. "You ready to talk about what got you in here?"

I laid back on my bunk and put my head behind my head. "I did some dumb shit. I got some money, got high and decided to drive around. I still had drugs in my pocket when I crashed into a car." I paused and took a deep breath. "I hit a mother and her kid. As far as I know, they both still alive."

I stopped talking for a minute. The words that I said hung in the air. I wished right then that I could get by. I was alone with my thoughts and Speedy. I didn't wanna come into there and get all soft but somehow the old man had got me to talk.

"Man look," Speedy said, "I ain't trying to tell you nothing but the truth. You may think you got control of that shit but it got control of you. You gotta change if you don't wanna be like me. You don't want your life to be like mine. Shit, I'm broke, old, alone, and in jail for the next however many years. You think I got a lot of life left in me? Nope."

I looked at Speedy in the eyes for a couple

of seconds. I don't know what it was about him that made me wanna talk to his ass but it was cool. He reminded me of my grandmother when I was younger, just someone real cool and easy to talk to. I wished I could wipe his words from my mind but I wouldn't be able to. I knew shit had to get better for me.

CHAPTER 9

Jericka

After Marco's little act, I chilled out for the rest of the night. I didn't know what else to do. We hadn't talked for the full two hours but he'd made me way more than I thought I'd end up with that night.

Later on that night when I pulled up outside of my complex, I got out of the car and walked to my apartment slowly. I wasn't in any kind of a rush to get inside there because I knew that I wasn't going home to anything. I'd thought about stopping by my mother's to grab Jasheem but I couldn't stop by that late and wake her up. I didn't know if she had to work the next day or not. Plus, I knew that if I went inside that she would know something was up and I didn't want to talk about it.

I walked into the house and just headed to my bedroom. I didn't bother turning on any of the lights cause there wasn't any point. It was just me and my thoughts. I hoped that everything went fine with Hov and his bail hearing. I wanted my baby to be out of jail already. It had only been a day but I knew that if he got locked up, he could end up doing some real time and I hoped that we could avoid that.

I took off my clothes and climbed into the bed. The other major thing that was on my mind was Marco. Something about him just had me thinking about him. I mean...he seemed to be the total package. He was sexy as hell, had money, good conversation, and recognized me for who I really was which was something that Hov had seemed to forget. I liked talking with Marco. It had been a long time since I felt someone genuinely cared like that outside of my usual circle of family and friends. I drifted off to sleep with Marco on my mind.

The room was dimly lit with red light. The high ceiling had to be at least 10 feet high. The walls went out in about six feet in either direction. There wasn't much room to move, especially with another person inside, but that was the way they wanted it to be. I walked into the room and closed and locked the door behind me. The only things in the room were a chair with a little table next to it. On top of the little table was a bottle of champagne and two glasses.

Marco was sitting in the chair. He was wearing a pair of black jeans and a white t-shirt. His muscles seemed to bulge. I walked over to him and bent over in front of him. I was dressed in an all-black swimsuit. The top had a gold ring between my breasts and the sides of the bottom had a gold ring on it. My skin and the swimsuit seemed to glow with the redness of the lights.

"You came here to look in the mirror, or you came to do something else?" Marco's deep voice filled up the room like he was speaking into a mic or something. It turned me on.

"I came to do something else," I said in a seductive tone.

I walked over to him and started dancing like I'd never danced before. It was some song that I'd never heard before, but somehow, I seemed to have moves to hit every beat that came with it. I was amazed at myself cause it was almost magical the way that I was moving.

I was doing all types of acrobatic shit that I'd never be able to do in real life.

When I was done, Marco looked at me and without him saying anything, we just knew that it was on. He stood up and walked up to me, backing me against the door. He grabbed me by my neck in a gentle way. He went ahead and bent my neck some and he started to lick and suck on it. He was real gentle with it all. I like every moment.

He turned my head back to the front and placed his soft, full lips on top of mine and kissed me. He was deep and passionate with it. His tongue and mine were licking one another's. I put my hand on his back and began to rub my hands over his soft skin. I kept raising my hand until I had his shirt halfway off. He stepped back and pulled it all the way off.

I had to take a couple of seconds to admire his body. His skin was clear and smooth but his muscles rippled like some shit I'd never seen before. He had one of them thug, prison bodies for real. I had never been the type to go the muscular dudes like that but Marco was definitely for me. He made a motion to try and step towards me but I held up my hand and put it on his chest to stop him.

"Hold up," I said. "Take those off too." I pointed to his pants and underwear. "You've already seen me naked. I think it's about time you return the favor."

"*You something else girl,*" he said. *He smirked at me and looked real sexy when he did it. I was mad turned on. I felt my pussy getting wet. I couldn't help it. I reached down into my panties and slowly put a finger inside of myself. I started playing with myself for a little bit and felt my thighs shake.*

"*Damn, that was sexy,*" Marco said. "*Come here.*"

I walked over to him and he grabbed my hand and held it up to his face. He shook his dreads out of the way before he took my hand and put my fingers into his mouth. He licked on each one that I'd had inside of me.

"*You taste good, Jericka,*" he said. *He picked me up and turned me around. Marco put me down in the chair. He grabbed me by the waist and pulled me so that I scooted to the end of the chair. Marco grabbed my panties and pulled them off of me slowly. He never broke eye contact with me when he did it. I tried to sit up and see his dick but I couldn't. When I tried to sit up further he pushed me back down.*

Once my panties were all the way off, Marco lowered himself right between my legs. I was going through some shit. It felt like I was high on some next level shit. It felt like his tongue was inches long and was hitting every single spot that I wanted it to. I moaned out loud and it felt like the whole room vibrated or some shit. Marco grabbed and palmed my ass. He pulled his tongue out of me just long enough to lick his thumb. He started to massage at my ass hole while he licked my pussy. It felt like magic or something the way he was making me feel.

When I felt like I couldn't take it anymore my whole body just shook with an orgasm that was so intense that I almost yelled. Instead, I moaned loudly. I couldn't believe that Marco had done all of that to my pussy and we hadn't even fucked.

"You ready?" Marco asked. He was sitting up and I could see him stroking his dick. The only problem was that I couldn't see the dick itself, only him jerking it off. I sat up but somehow managed to fall out of the chair.

I woke up in my bed, confused like shit. It took me a couple of seconds before I realized that I had been dreaming. It took my ass a couple more seconds to realize that it was little wet between my legs. My dream had felt so real that I'd managed to get myself wet in my sleep. How could one conversation with one dude on time have me so stuck?

I looked at the clock. I was surprised that I'd slept the five hours straight. I hopped out of my bed and headed to the bathroom. I brushed my teeth, washed my face, threw on some clothes and I was out the door to my car. I had to go and pick up Jasheem.

I got to my mother's house and used my key to let myself inside. I headed into the kitchen but didn't see either of them. When I went into the living room I saw them both sitting on the couch. My mother was looking at something on her phone and Jasheem was watching Pokemon, his favorite cartoon.

"Why you come rushing in here like somebody chasing you?" She asked. She looked concerned. Even Jasheem looked up at me.

"I thought you had to work this morning," I said in a huff. I sat down in the chair and took a breath. I held out my hands and Jasheem walked over to me and climbed into my lap. I kissed him on the forehead and he put his head on me.

"Don't you remember that you asked me if I had to work or not before you went to work?" my mother said. "I told you no. Where's your head at girl?" She rolled her eyes at me.

I felt myself get emotional right there. I had so many places for my head to be at. All this shit was swirling through my mind. I had thoughts about Hov, Marco, everything. I wondered how was it that I'd let my shit get like that. I wanted to tell my mother about it but I couldn't. She and I were close for sure but I didn't wanna admit all of that to her. It was my own shame.

"Jericka, what's wrong?" my mother asked when I didn't say anything back to her.

"Nothing ma," I said. "I'll call you later. I gotta go." I told Jasheem to grab his stuff and I headed to the front door. I waited for him there and my mother walked in.

"Now look, you're grown and all that and you can always make your own decision but I'm your mother. I'm gonna be here regardless of anything. You gotta know that by now," my mother said.

I just nodded at her while Jasheem walked over to me. I opened the door and he headed towards the car. I kissed my mother on the cheek and walked out heading towards the car.

I got in the car and drove off, heading home. The thing was though...I didn't really wanna go home. Hov not being there was definitely weighing heavy on my mind. I didn't wanna be in the house if he wasn't there. When I stopped at a red light, I called Tamika.

"Hey girl," I said. "What you doing today?"

"What's up? I ain't doing nothing. I was gonna work but I called out," she said. "I just feel like chilling out today. You?"

"Oh ok," I said.

"What?"

"I just got a lot of stuff on my mind and I was wondering if you wanted some company but I don't wanna get all in your spot if you trying to just chill out today," I said.

"Oh please bitch," she said. "That means I ain't dealing with friends today. You and Jasheem are family. Come over when you want to."

"Thanks," I said as I turned the car. "I appreciate it. See you in a few."

I turned the car and drove to headed towards Tamika's house. Jasheem must have still been tired because he'd drifted off to sleep in his car seat. About ten minutes later, we got to Tamika's house. He was still sleeping so I just brought him inside and put him into her bed.

"You just picked him up from your mother's house?" Tamika asked when I came back into the living room.

"Yeah," I said.

"How was work last night?" Tamika asked.

She headed into the kitchen and pulled out a bottle of champagne and some orange juice.

"Damn girl, you trying to drink already? It's barely ten in the morning," I said with a laugh.

She brought over all the stuff for the mimosas. "Oh well. You got shit you going through. You could use a drink. Plus, it's something light so it's not gonna do much."

"I guess," I said. She poured me out some champagne.

"Is that enough?" She asked.

"A little bit more," I said with a smile. She busted out laughing and made mine nice and strong, just the way I liked it.

"So how was work?" She repeated her question.

"Well it was good," I said. "Shit, it was better than good. I made a lot of money."

"Oh word? That's good," she said.

"There was something else too," I told her as I sipped my drink.

"What?" she asked.

"I met a guy," I said.

"Well duh," she said. "It's a strip club."

"Nah, not like that," I said. "I mean I met a guy who seems like he could be something."

She narrowed her eyes. "Something like what?"

"Girl I don't know. He was just...everything," I said. "His name was Marco. When I hit the stage, I thought he fell in love or something. He was tipping like crazy. He was throwing mad money at me."

"Get outta here," she said. "Go off! That should help you with Hov's bail and hopefully you'll have some left to save."

"I hope so," I said.

"What else happened?" Tamika asked. She sat back in her arm chair and looked at me. She was clearly ready to get the tea from me.

"Girl, we went to the back for a private dance," I said.

"Oh my God," she said. Her eyes got all wide. "Oh shit! You fucked him? You fucked him!" She got all excited and a mischievous grin came across her face.

"Hell no," I said loudly. "And keep your voice down girl. You know Jasheem ain't no dummy. I don't need him hearing that and repeating it to his father."

"My bad," she said. "So if you ain't fuck him, why you acting all secretive?"

"Mika, there was something about this dude," I said. "He was everything I'd look for and nothing I'd look for at the same time. He was tall, handsome, beautiful skin and a dread head."

"Yes! A dread head? Mmm...I bet he got a big dick too," she said. "How was the lap dance?"

"I barely danced," I said. "He paid for mad time up front and I danced for a little bit and we ended up just talking for most of it. He told me a little about him and I told him about Hov."

"You told him about Hov? Hmm...I never known you to chat about Hov like that," she frowned.

"I know," I said. "There was something about him though. I don't know what it was at all but I like him. At the end of the night he tipped me $100 and gave me his number. He told me that when I was ready to stop messing with a lame that I should call him."

Tamika finished her drink in a gulp and poured another. "Wow, so what you gonna do?"

"I don't know," I said honestly. "What you think I should do?"

"I think you should call him," she said. I was kind of shocked that she said that.

"Why?" I asked. I was curious. She needed to put it into some kind of context or something. Was she trying to get me to cheat on Hov?

"Jericka, you know how bad things with you and Hov are," she said. "You know that he ain't gonna get better until you make him get better. The only way for Hov to get better is for you to leave him. He ain't gonna do it knowing that you always there to hold him down. Besides, it sounds like this Marco dude got you kinda open. Why not explore it? If he's trying to do right by you and Jasheem, why not let him?"

I sat back and let her words wash over me. It was true what she was saying. I guess it wouldn't hurt me at all to at least just give him a call and hear him out. Maybe that was what I'd do.

CHAPTER 10

Hov

"Where the fuck is this bitch at?" I mumbled the words out loud to myself. I had been trying to get a hold of Jericka all morning long but she wasn't answering any of my calls. It was now the afternoon. I'd been calling her ass all morning long and she hadn't answered. Every time I called, it just kept going to voicemail. I didn't know what types of games she was trying to play but I wasn't with the shits at all.

"Hi, you've reached Jericka. Please leave me a message and I'll get back to you. Peace and love," the phone beeped. I'd lost count of how many times I'd called her. I was pissed the fuck off.

"Jericka baby, I don't know why your phone keeps going to voicemail but I'll give you a call later on. My bail hearing is set for Monday. I want you to try and make it if you can but if not I'll call you and tell you. Look, you gotta make as much money as you can this weekend. I'm not trying to be in here passed Tue—" The phone cut off in the middle of my message asking me if I was complete. I hung up the phone, now even more annoyed than I was before.

I was pissed off cause it seemed like we might have finally reached our breaking point. Jericka had never not answered the phone like this before. Had she really waited till I needed her most for her to crack under the pressure? Nah, it couldn't be. I needed her to hold me down and make sure that I didn't stay locked up. She'd been a ride or die for too long for her to just give up on your boy now.

I needed to send someone to her spot to look for her. I called some of my old crew, the ones I still fucked with at least. I called up a couple of them but nobody was answering their phone.

The ones who I was at least able to make a call to had their phones set up so they couldn't take collect calls.

I decided to call up my nigga James. I knew that I could count on him. I just hoped his ass wasn't high cause then I'd never be able to get any help out of him. He picked up after a couple of rings.

"Yo? Wassup my guy? How you dealing with the inside?" James asked. James always had his ear to the street so it made sense that he would know that I was locked up.

"I'm good," I said. "You know me, too tough to break." I was putting up a front. It had only been like two days but I was starting to need a fix bad. I was trying to hide it cause I didn't want the dudes inside to know how bad my problem had gotten but it was starting to get worse.

"I feel you," he said.

"You got a pen on you?" I asked him.

"Yeah, why?"

"Here, write down Jericka's number. I want you to call it for me. If it goes to voicemail then I want you to stop by my crib," I explained.

"And what you want me to say?"

"I want you to tell her that she needs to be picking up my calls," I said to him.

"Aight, I got you," James said. "I'll holla at you. Call later if you can. I'll go handle this for you now."

"Appreciate it," I said before I hung up the phone.

I headed back to my cell, sulking all the way. There was nothing like being away from the people you cared about. I hated that feeling. Not to mention that I felt like Jericka wasn't taking care of home the way that I felt she should be.

I got back into my cell right before the next count. Speedy was already in there, doing pushups on the floor. He must have noticed my mood cause he stopped when he saw me come in.

"What's wrong with you now, young blood? You always got a frown on your face," he said.

"Man, my shorty not answering the phone," I said as I sat down on my bunk. "Shit don't make no sense."

"I mean…there might be a reason," he said. I just looked at him, waiting for him to explain. "When I got locked up the first time…like for real locked up, my family left me. My wife took my kids. First she went to her sister's, but after that she just moved on. She brought them to see me on time and that was it."

"Jericka ain't like that," I said. "We been together forever."

"Nah man, you ain't listen to nothin' I said to you," he said. "You chose that shit over her. You think I don't see it in your eyes? You about to start going through withdrawals real bad. You got a real problem Hov. But maybe that's what you need. That's what had to happen to me a couple of times before I stayed clean for a long ass time. You gotta go through the withdrawals and shit so that you can finally figure out how you gonna get clean."

~

Jericka

Jasheem and I spent the rest of the day at Tamika's. We got out of the house and headed to the mall where we got some frozen yogurt and stuff. It was cool to just relax and kick it with Tamika, especially when I had all that other stress going on.

I was laying in my bed, watching TV when I remembered that I had Marco's number. I reached into my wallet, glad that I hadn't spent the bill that he wrote his number on. I pulled out my cell phone.

I wondered if I should call. I didn't know what would happen if I did but I decided that it was worth it. "Fuck it," I said.

I dialed the number and after three rings, a familiar, deep voice picked up.

"Hello?"

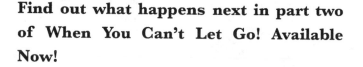

Find out what happens next in part two of When You Can't Let Go! Available Now!

To find out when Mia Black has new books available, **follow Mia Black on Instagram: @authormiablack**

WHEN YOU CAN'T LET GO 2

Marco knows what to say and what to do to get Jericka's attention, but she's not sure his intentions are real. She's seen her fair share of guys who flash their money around like it means nothing to them.

Life with Hov continues to spiral out of control. As things get worse at home, she questions her feelings about the man she's loved for so long and the man who has piqued her curiosity. Maybe Marco is not as bad as she thought. Before she has time to absorb those thoughts, she learns that Hov has gotten himself in another situation. She does what she always does for him, but that kind gesture doesn't protect her from what comes next.

Find out what happens in part two of When You Can't Let Go!

Follow Mia Black on Instagram for more updates: @authormiablack